To Jon and Tom - M.M. and N.S.

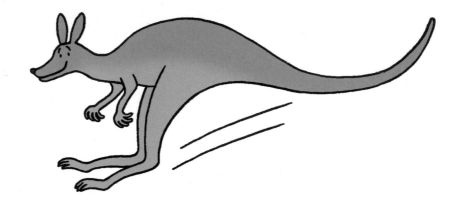

First published 2010 by Macmillan Children's Books
This edition published 2011 by Macmillan Children's Books
a division of Macmillan Publishers Limited
20 New Wharf Road, London N1 9RR
Basingstoke and Oxford
Associated companies throughout the world
www.panmacmillan.com

ISBN: 978-0-330-51229-9
Text copyright © Michaela Morgan 2010
Illustrations copyright © Nick Sharratt 2010
Moral rights asserted.

3 5 7 9 8 6 4

A CIP catalogue for this book is available from the British Library.

Printed in Belgium

NEVER SHAKE A RATTLESNAKE

Written by Michaela Morgan

Illustrated by Nick Sharratt

MACMILLAN CHILDREN'S BOOKS

You should never tuck **piranhas** inside your best pyjamas.

Don't try to knit a scarf for an extra-tall giraffe

and don't ever EVER pat a **porcupine.**

You should never style the hair
of a grumpy grizzly bear.

STYLING MOUSSE

You should never NEVER shake a rattlesnake.

Don't nest up high in trees

with the **hairy** chimpanzees

and don't try to keep
a whale in a **lake**.

Don't lend your **hat** and **coat** to a goat.

Don't try to dress a fox
in frilly bonnet
and pink socks

and don't EVER take
a **rhino** on a boat.

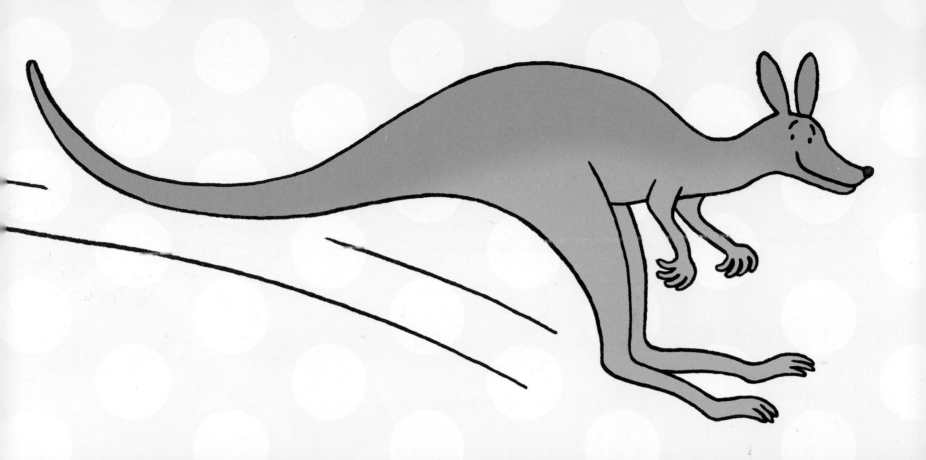

DON'T keep a chameleon in the **dark.**

and don't leave tiny dogs
out in the **breeze**.

Don't buy **fancy** shoes for camels . . .

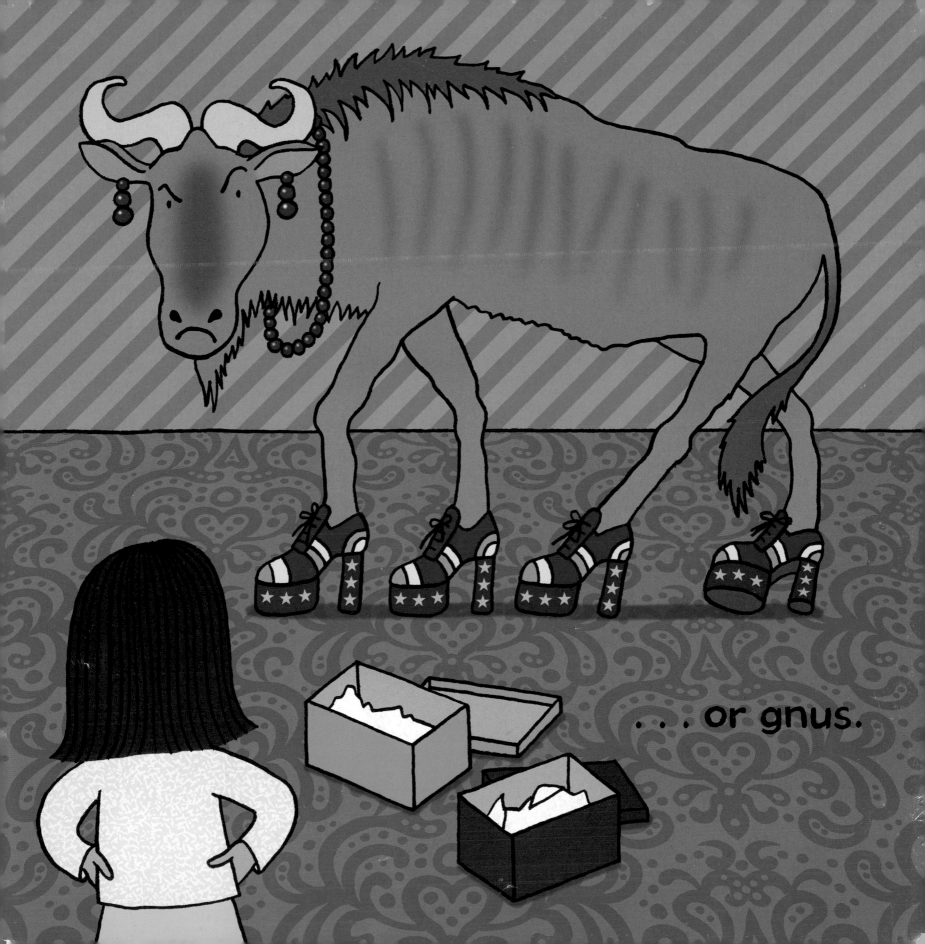

. . . or gnus.

and never

never